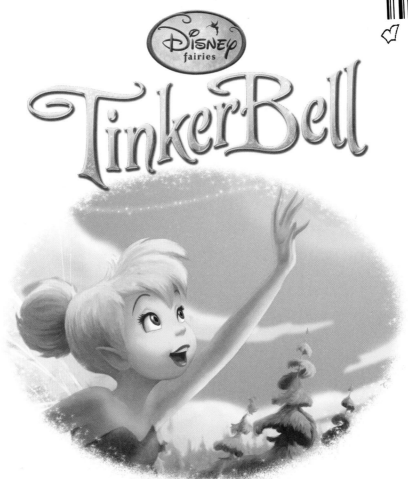

Tinker Bell's Scratch & Sniff Surprises

By Andrea Posner-Sanchez

Illustrated by the Disney Storybook Artists

Random House 🏠 New York

Copyright © 2009 Disney Enterprises, Inc. All rights reserved. Published in the United States by Random House Children's Books, a division of Random House, Inc., 1745 Broadway, New York, NY 10019, and in Canada by Random House of Canada Limited, Toronto, in conjunction with Disney Enterprises, Inc. Random House and colophon are registered trademarks of Random House, Inc.
Library of Congress Control Number: 2008932772
ISBN: 978-0-7364-2590-2
www.randomhouse.com/kids
Printed in the United States of America
10 9 8 7 6 5 4 3 2 1   First Edition

This is Pixie Hollow. From the moment Tinker Bell arrived here, she knew she was going to love it. Everything looks— and smells—so magical!

Tink loves how Pixie Hollow smells like winter, spring, summer, and fall—all rolled into one. That's because Pixie Hollow is the only place in the world where all four seasons exist at the same time!

Scratch and sniff the fresh air.

Tinker Bell lives and works in Tinkers' Nook, along with the other tinker fairies. Everyone here is always busy fixing and building all sorts of useful objects!

Tink even fixes her own clothes. When her leaf dresses are too big, she trims them so that they fit just right. Tink doesn't mind the work—she's happy to have such nice-smelling outfits!

Scratch and sniff the leaf dress.

Tinker Bell and her friends help deliver supplies to the nature fairies. Usually, the deliveries go off without a hitch. But sometimes, Sprinting Thistles knock Tink's wagon right off its path! Tink learned quickly that these weeds are fast, dangerous—and stinky!

Scratch and sniff the Sprinting Thistle . . .
   if you dare.

Terence is a dust-keeper. Tink and the other fairies wouldn't be able to fly without their daily dose of pixie dust. Tinker Bell is always nicely surprised when Terence first pours the sparkly, sweet-scented dust over her head!

Scratch and sniff the pixie dust.

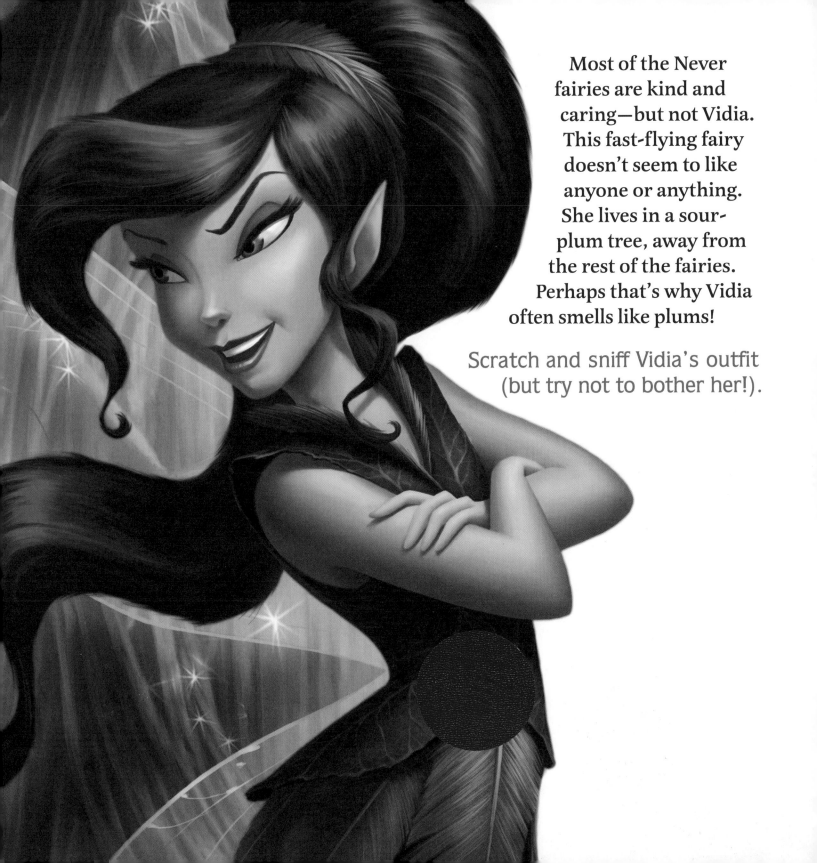

Most of the Never fairies are kind and caring—but not Vidia. This fast-flying fairy doesn't seem to like anyone or anything. She lives in a sour-plum tree, away from the rest of the fairies. Perhaps that's why Vidia often smells like plums!

Scratch and sniff Vidia's outfit (but try not to bother her!).

The Never fairies get along well with most of the wildlife in Pixie Hollow. But the hawks that often fly above the pine tree forest would rather eat the fairies than play with them!

Scratch and sniff the pine tree.

Luckily, scout fairies are always on the lookout, armed
with raspberries for protection!

Cheese the mouse eats so much cheese, he actually smells like cheese! When he's not helping pull a supply wagon for the tinkers, he's looking for cheese. No cheese here, but he does find Tinker Bell's collection of Lost Things!

Scratch and sniff Cheese.

Fairies are responsible for painting flowers, leaves, and even ladybugs. The paint is made from the juice of berries. Ladybug spots are made from blackberry juice. These bugs smell as good as they look!

Scratch and sniff the ladybug.

The Everblossom opens its fragrant petals and gives off a golden glow. That means it's time for the Never fairies to bring springtime to the mainland!

Scratch and sniff
the Everblossom!